ABOUT THE BANK STREET READY-TO-READ SERIES

Seventy years of educational research and innovative teaching have given the Bank Street College of Education the reputation as America's most trusted name in early childhood education.

Because no two children are exactly alike in their development, we have designed the *Bank Street Ready-to-Read* series in three levels to accommodate the individual stages of reading readiness of children ages four through eight.

- ● *Level 1:* GETTING READY TO READ—read-alouds for children who are taking their first steps toward reading.
- ● *Level 2:* READING TOGETHER—for children who are just beginning to read by themselves but may need a little help.
- ○ *Level 3:* I CAN READ IT MYSELF—for children who can read independently.

Our three levels make it easy to select the books most appropriate for a child's development and enable him or her to grow with the series step by step. The *Bank Street Ready-to-Read* books also overlap and reinforce each other, further encouraging the reading process.

We feel that making reading fun and enjoyable is the single most important thing that you can do to help children become good readers. And we hope you'll be a part of Bank Street's long tradition of learning through sharing.

The Bank Street College of Education

In honor of the Altman sneeze
—E.L.S.
To Valentino
—G.F.

I LOVE TO SNEEZE

A Bantam Little Rooster Book/August 1992

Little Rooster is a trademark of Bantam Books,
a division of Bantam Doubleday Dell Publishing Group, Inc.

Series graphic design by Alex Jay/Studio J

Special thanks to James A. Levine, Betsy Gould,
Diane Arico, and Susan Schwarzchild.

Library of Congress Cataloging-in-Publication Data

Schecter, Ellen.
I love to sneeze/by Ellen Schecter;
illustrated by Gioia Fiammenghi.
p. cm. — (Bank Street ready-to-read)
"A Byron Preiss book."
"A Bantam little rooster book."
Summary: A lover of sneezes describes
the havoc wrought by such nasal explosions,
which have the power to blow the whiskers off
the cat and make freckles jump noses.
ISBN 0-553-07576-4. — ISBN 0-553-35159-1 (pbk.)
[1. Sneeze—Fiction. 2. Stories in rhyme.] I. Fiammenghi, Gioia, ill.
II. Title. III. Series.
PZ8.3.S321al 1992
[E]—dc20
91-28551 CIP AC

Published simultaneously in the United States and Canada

Bantam Books are published by Bantam Books, a division of Bantam Doubleday Dell
Publishing Group, Inc. Its trademark, consisting of the words "Bantam Books" and the
portrayal of a rooster, is Registered in U.S. Patent and Trademark Office and in other
countries. Marca Registrada. Bantam Books, 666 Fifth Avenue, New York, New York 10103.

PRINTED IN THE UNITED STATES OF AMERICA

0 9 8 7 6 5 4 3 2 1

Bank Street Ready-to-Read™

I Love to Sneeze

by Ellen Schecter
Illustrated by Gioia Fiammenghi

A Byron Preiss Book

A BANTAM LITTLE ROOSTER BOOK
NEW YORK · TORONTO · LONDON · SYDNEY · AUCKLAND

Ahhh! I love to sneeze!
I throw back my head
and bend my knees.
I take a deep breath.

I can't say no.
I cover my mouth
and then I let go—
Ah—Ahh—Ahhh—CHOO!

But whenever I sneeze
ice cubes unfreeze.
Lampshades go sailing
into the breeze.

Cups go flying,
and carpets, and keys.
I even scramble
the ABCs.

My sneeze blows the whiskers
clean off the cat.
It irons the sheets
even and flat.

Phones lose their ring.
Jars start to jog.
My sneeze blows the fleas
right off the dog.

My sneeze scares the buzz
out of the bees.
It blows all the leaves
back on the trees.

My sneeze sends the swings
on a sky ride
and blows all the children
back up the slide.

17

My sneeze blows the baseball
back to the bat.
It knocks all the letters
right off my hat.

It blasts the umpires
up to the skies
and splatters the ketchup
off my french fries.

My sneeze knocks the clowns
out of their socks
and makes Jack jump
back into his box.

Stripes peel off zebras.
Horses go flying.
One tiny sneeze starts
the crocodiles crying.

My sneeze makes the roosters
crow out of tune
and blows all the cows
over the moon.

One little sneeze
and the ducks lose
their quacks.
My sneeze plucks the feathers
right off their backs.

My sneeze dries the seas,
turns the moon
to green cheese,
makes the octopus squeeze
and tickles the keys,

makes butter fly,
makes freckles jump noses,
and blows the red
out of the roses.

Ahhh! I love to sneeze!
I throw back my head
and bend my knees.
I take a deep breath.
I can't say no.
I cover my mouth
and then I let go—
Ah—Ahh—Ahhh—CHOO!

Excuse me, please!
I just love to sneeze!

32